STAR WARS®

THE PHANTOM MENACE

Adapted by Courtney Carbone

Illustrated by Heather Martinez

 A GOLDEN BOOK • NEW YORK

randomhousekids.com

ISBN 978-0-7364-3542-0 (trade) — ISBN 978-0-7364-3543-7 (ebook)

Printed in the United States of America

10 9 8

A long time ago in a galaxy far, far away . . .

The peaceful planet of Naboo is under a blockade from the greedy Trade Federation! The Galactic Republic quickly sends **Qui-Gon Jinn** and **Obi-Wan Kenobi** to help. They are Jedi Knights, guardians of justice and masters of the **Force**—a power that connects all living things.

But when Qui-Gon and Obi-Wan arrive, they are attacked by battle droids! The Jedi defend themselves with their **lightsabers**, but they are outnumbered and must flee the Trade Federation battleship.

On Naboo, Qui-Gon and Obi-Wan
meet a funny creature
named **Jar Jar Binks**.

Jar Jar takes them to the underwater city of the Gungans.

The Gungan leader, **Boss Nass**, does not want to help Qui-Gon and Obi-Wan with their mission. But Boss Nass gives them a submarine and allows Jar Jar to guide the Jedi to the royal palace of Naboo. On their way through the planet's core, they are attacked by **giant** sea creatures!

After a narrow escape, the heroes arrive at the royal palace. **Queen Amidala** is being held **hostage** by the leader of the Trade Federation, Viceroy Gunray!

The Jedi quickly free Queen Amidala and her handmaidens. They race aboard the queen's royal starship and **blast off** for Coruscant, the capital of the Republic, to get help.

Oh, no! Federation vulture droids attack the royal starship! A team of astromech droids hurries to repair the ship's shields. A brave droid named **R2-D2** saves the day!

Across the galaxy, the true villain behind the Federation's plot is furious that Queen Amidala has escaped! Darth Sidious is a Sith Lord—an evil master of the dark side of the Force. **Darth Sidious** orders his apprentice, **Darth Maul**, to find Queen Amidala at once.

The royal starship's hyperdrive is damaged, so the heroes land on the desert planet Tatooine to make repairs. Qui-Gon, Obi-Wan, and Queen Amidala's handmaiden, **Padmé**, find a new hyperdrive in a local junk shop. But they don't have money to pay Watto the junk dealer.

Padmé meets **Anakin Skywalker**, a slave boy who works in the shop. Anakin can fix anything—and he is a skilled podracer!

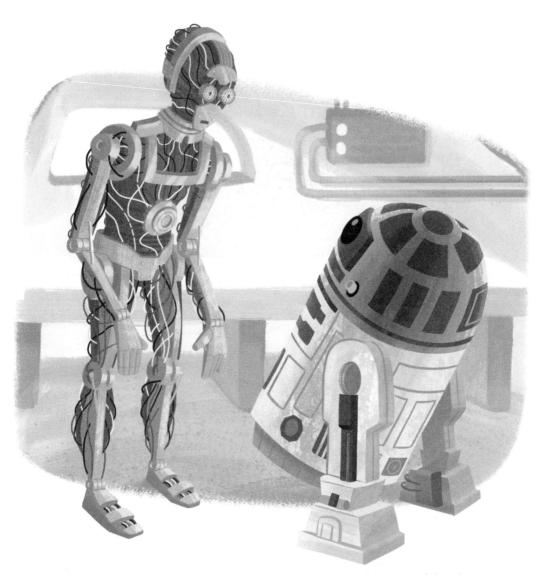

A sandstorm blows in, so Anakin brings his new friends to his house. They meet his mother, Shmi, and a droid that Anakin is building. "Hello, my name is **C-3PO**," the droid says.

Qui-Gon senses that the Force is strong in the boy. He thinks Anakin could become a Jedi!

Qui-Gon makes a bet with Watto. If Anakin places first in the next podrace, Qui-Gon wins the hyperdrive—and the boy's **freedom**. But if the boy loses, Watto wins the queen's royal starship.

During the podrace, Anakin zips and **ZOOMS** past the competition. The crowd goes wild when he crosses the finish line first!

Soon the royal starship is repaired. Anakin is sad to leave his mother but excited to begin his Jedi training.

Suddenly, Darth Maul launches a sneak attack! Qui-Gon fights bravely, giving the heroes enough time to blast off for Coruscant.

When they arrive on Coruscant, Queen Amidala asks the Republic Senate for help while Qui-Gon brings Anakin before the **Jedi Council**. He wants the boy to become a Jedi.

Yoda, a powerful Jedi Master, worries that Anakin has fear in his heart. And fear can cause a Jedi to turn to the **dark side** of the Force. "Clouded this boy's future is . . . ," Yoda says.

The Republic refuses to help Queen Amidala, so the
heroes return to Naboo to save her people. They ask the
Gungans to form an alliance. Padmé reveals that she is really
Queen Amidala in **disguise**! Padmé begs Boss Nass to
help, and he agrees. They will all fight the Federation together!

Padmé, Anakin, and the Jedi sneak into the palace. They release the Naboo pilots, who **blast off** in starfighters and attack the Federation fleet in space. Suddenly, **Darth Maul** appears! Qui-Gon and Obi-Wan face the villain as Padmé and her guards race off to capture the viceroy.

Outside the palace, Jar Jar and the Gungans battle the Trade Federation army.

But the Gungans are outnumbered—and their shields
are no match for thousands of **battle droids**!

To stay safe, Anakin is hiding in an empty Naboo starfighter with R2-D2. All of a sudden, the starfighter takes off on autopilot—sending Anakin into the middle of a space battle! Anakin uses his amazing podracing skills to fly into the droid control ship—and **blow it up**!

Ka-boom! Without the control ship powering them, the battle droids all over Naboo shut down.

In the palace, the Jedi fight Darth Maul together. But the Sith Lord is driven by the **power** of anger and hate. Darth Maul strikes Qui-Gon down with his double-sided lightsaber and knocks Obi-Wan into a deep pit. Just when it seems that Obi-Wan is defeated, the Jedi springs into action and destroys Darth Maul with one **mighty** blow!

Obi-Wan runs to his master's side. With his **last breath**, Qui-Gon asks Obi-Wan to train Anakin as a Jedi.

The Federation has been **defeated**! Padmé Amidala, Boss Nass, and the people of Naboo celebrate their return to peace.

Obi-Wan keeps his promise to Qui-Gon and vows to teach Anakin in the ways of the **Force**.

Anakin's journey to become a Jedi has begun!